ISBN 0-590-46284-9

Text copyright © 1985 by Richard Buckley.
Illustrations copyright © 1985 by Eric Carle.
All rights reserved. Published by Scholastic Inc.,
730 Broadway, New York, NY 10003, by arrangement with
Picture Book Studio, USA, an imprint of Neugebauer Press USA Inc.

12 11 10 9 8 7 6 5 4 3 2 1   2 3 4 5 6 7/9

Printed in the U.S.A.   08

First Scholastic printing, October 1992

The Greedy Python

The Greedy Python

SCHOLASTIC INC.

New York Toronto London Auckland Sydney

Half-hidden in the jungle green
The biggest snake there's ever been
Wound back and forth and in between.

The giant snake was very strong
And very, very, very long.
He had a monstrous appetite,
His stomach stretched from left to right.

He quickly gobbled in one bite
Whatever creature came in sight:
A mouse that scampered to and fro,
A frog that jumped up from below,
A bat that hung from his left toe,
A fish that swam a bit too slow,
A bird that flew a bit too low.

A porcupine still half asleep,
A monkey who was in mid-leap,

A leopard sitting in a tree,
A buffalo who came to see.

An elephant, complete with trunk,
Was swallowed in a single chunk.
"I'm far too big to eat!" he cried.
"Oh no you're not!" the snake replied.

At last the python's meal was done
And he lay resting in the sun.
The animals inside his skin
Were making quite a dreadful din;

And when they all began to kick
The snake began to feel quite sick.

He coughed the whole lot up again —
Each one of them — and there were ten.

He soon felt better, and what's more
Was hungrier than just before.
He hadn't learned a single thing:

His greed was quite astonishing.
He saw his own tail, long and curved,
And thought that lunch was being served.

He closed his jaws on his own rear
Then swallowed hard… and disappeared!

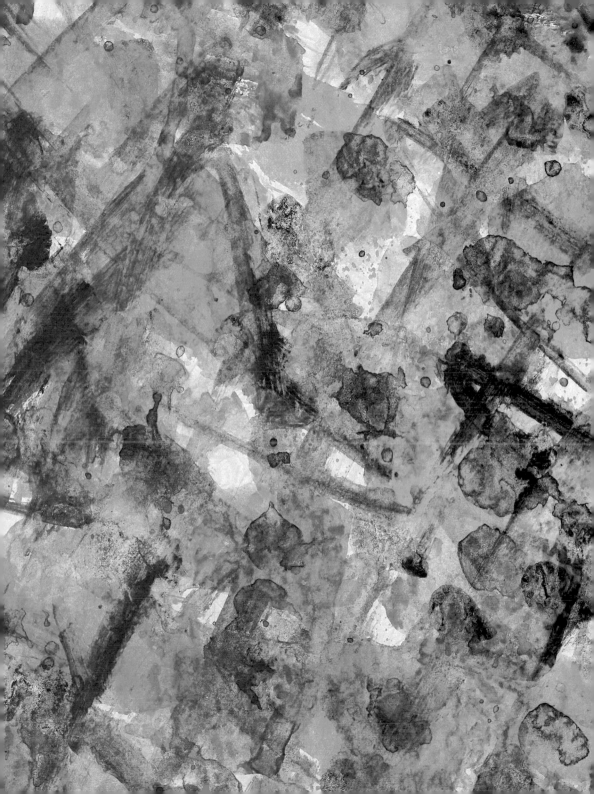

Born in Syracuse, N.Y. in 1929, ERIC CARLE moved to Germany in 1935 with his parents. His schooling there included work under Ernst Schneidler at the Academy of Graphic Arts. He returned to America in 1952 and worked as a graphic designer for the New York Times, and later as art director for an international advertising agency. His first two books, 1,2,3 TO THE ZOO (1968), and THE VERY HUNGRY CATERPILLAR (1969), gained him immediate international recognition. The latter title, now considered a modern classic, has sold over 4 million copies and been translated into 14 languages.

He writes of his work: "When I first began to think about children's books, it reawakened in me struggles of my own childhood, touching an unfinished area of my own growing up. A child spends five years basically at home — a place of warmth, play and protection. Then school begins, and all of a sudden it is a world of schedule, abstraction, and organized learning. Very simply put, I decided I wanted to create books that make this transition easier."